CAT the CAT Who Is THAT?

by
MO WILLEMS

Balzer + Bray

An Imprint of HarperCollins Publishers

Cat the Cat, who is that?

It's Mouse the Mouse!

Hi, Mouse the Mouse!

Cat the Cat, who is that?

It's Duck the Duck!

Hi, Duck the Duck!

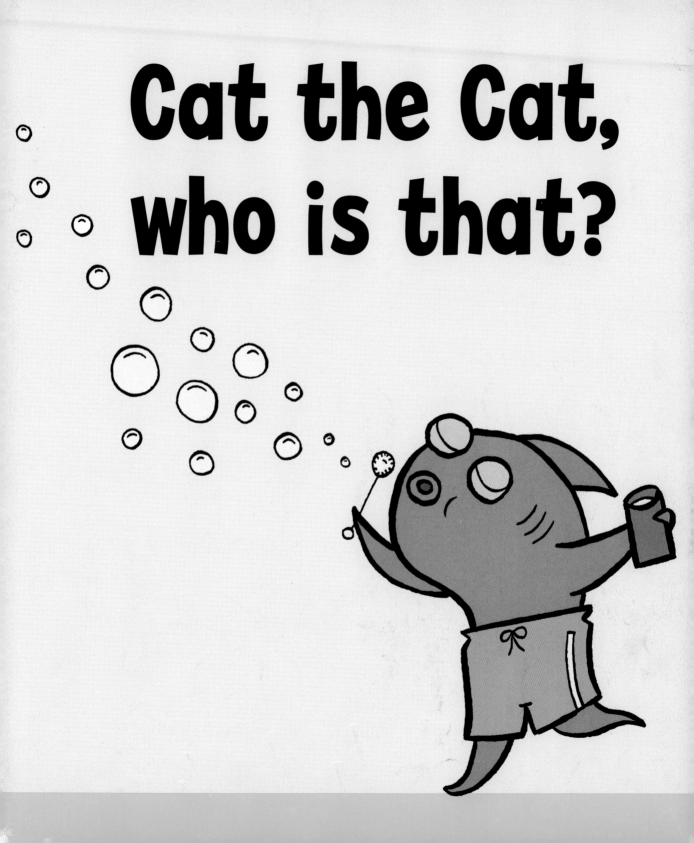

It's Fish the Fish!

Hi, Fish the Fish!

Cat the Cat

likes her friends!

Cat the Cat, who is THAT?

To my wife, Cher.
Blarggie! Blarggie!

Cat the Cat, Who Is THAT?
Copyright © 2010 by Mo Willems
Manufactured in China.

Library of Congress Cataloging-in-Publication Data
Willems, Mo.
   Cat the cat, who is that? / Mo Willems. — 1st ed.
      p.   cm.
   Summary: An exuberant cat introduces readers to her friends.
   ISBN 978-0-06-172840-2 (trade bdg.) — ISBN 978-0-06-172841-9 (lib. bdg.)
   [1. Cats—Fiction. 2. Animals—Fiction. 3. Friendship—Fiction.] I. Title.
PZ7.W65535Cat 2010   2008046187
[E]—dc22   CIP
                                                     AC

Typography by Martha Rago
15 16 17 18 19 20 SCP 10 9 8 7 6 5

First Edition